TERRY DEARY

GREEK TALES

THE LION'S SLAVE

Inside illustrations by Helen Flook

BLOOMSBURY EDUCATION
AN IMPRINT OF BLOOMSBURY
LONDON OXFORD NEW YORK NEW DELHI SYDNEY

INTRODUCTION

Syracuse, 213 BCE

Aesop the Greek storyteller said: *You may share the work of the great, but you will not share the rewards.*

My master liked to call me stupid. "You are stupid, Lydia," he would say. "If you had twice as many brains, you'd be a half-wit."

That was a clever thing to say. But then my master, Archimedes, was the cleverest man in the whole of Greece. So if he called me stupid, then I must have been.

I cleaned his rooms...

and washed his clothes...

cooked his meals...

and helped him test his machines.

Because Archimedes was a great inventor, they called him the Lion of Syracuse. And he often roared at me like a lion.

"I bet your brain feels as good as new, seeing that you've never used it," he told me.

"Thank you, Sir," I said.

And I was clumsy. When I tried to dust the bottles and jars in his workshop, I often spilled them.

"You are a donkey, Lydia. What are you?"

"A donkey, Sir," I said.

There was a story about Archimedes taking a bath one day, long before I went to work for him. He lay in the bath and the water overflowed.

That gave him an idea – some maths idea I've never understood. Anyway, Archimedes jumped out of the bath and ran down the street calling out the news.

"Eureka*!" he cried. "I have found it! Eureka! I have found the answer!"

But Archimedes hadn't stopped to put on any clothes!

* Of course, you know *eureka* is Ancient Greek for "I have found it". "Eureka!" was one of Archimedes' favourite cries.

He forgot about simple things like that. And I reckon it was his brilliant brain that got him killed.

He thought everyone was as excited by his inventions as he was. He forgot that people have feelings. Feelings of revenge.

If he'd been as stupid as me then he'd still be alive today.

It all started when the Romans came to Syracuse...

CHAPTER 1

"You are stupid, Lydia, stupid," Archimedes told me. "I don't know why I hired you. You must be a very cheap servant."

"I am more than cheap – you don't pay me anything at all," I reminded him.

"Then how do you live?"

"I eat a little of the food I cook for you and I sleep on a straw bed in an attic room."

"Huh!" he grumbled. "Then I still pay you too much."

"Yes, Sir," I said.

And on that day, the Romans arrived to attack us. Their ships lay in the cool, blue sea off the shore of Syracuse. Soldiers stood on the decks, but didn't dare to land just yet. Our soldiers on the walls would have shot them with their arrows.

"Will the Romans kill us when they land, Sir?" I asked.

"Stupid child," Archimides said. "You, Lydia, are a young and healthy girl. They will not kill you. You are not worth it. They will take you away and make you a slave. But then you will not have a kind master like me, will you?"

"No, Sir," I said.

Archimedes' house stood on the top of a hill. We could look over the garden walls and down over the city walls to see

the Roman fleet shimmering in the heat.
The sun beat down on us and I wished I
could swim in that cool, blue sea.

"I would like to smash those ships,"
Archimedes said.

"You could throw rocks at them," I suggested.

He looked at me and mopped his bald, sweating head with a cloth. "Stupid girl," he said.

"Can you do something about them?" I asked.

"Perhaps I could... I could invent something," he said.

I clapped my hands and jumped on the dry, brown grass. "That would be marvellous, Sir. You are a wonderful inventor. You invented a way to raise water out of a river and into the fields."

"Yes," he nodded. "They call it Archimedes' screw."

"I'm sure you could invent a machine to fire big rocks at those ships," I said.

My master shook his head. "Find me a rock and I'll show you why it's not possible."

There were no rocks in the garden because I kept it weeded and full of flowers. But there were some large ones in the field outside the garden wall.

"I'll get one from the field," I said.

Archimedes threw up his hands. "Silly child. Those stones are too large for you to carry."

"Then I'll throw one over the wall," I offered.

"If you can't pick it up, you can't throw it!" He roared his lion roar.

"Oh, throwing it is easier!" I laughed. Then I picked up the plank of wood that my master used as a garden seat, tucked it under my arm and walked out into the field.

I placed the plank on a round stone and let one end drop onto the ground.

I rolled a large rock onto that end. Then I jumped onto the other end. The rock shot up into the air.

I remember it to this day.

I remember the way my master Archimedes screamed...

CHAPTER 2

The rock soared into the cloudless sky, looped over the wall and headed down into the garden. At least it *would* have headed into the garden if my master hadn't been standing there. Instead, it sort of headed for his head.

Handsome young Ajax, who lives in the main street, has fine hair that is parted in the middle. My master doesn't have hair on his head. If he *had*, the rock would have parted it. Instead, it almost parted his head – and then all those fine brains would have spilled out onto the dusty grass and spoiled my fine flowers.

But Archimedes ducked and scrambled out of the way and the rock landed with a thump on the grass.

"Oooops!" I said with a silly grin. "Sorry, Sir!"

He didn't call me stupid – he was spluttering and moaning too much to call me anything. I brought the plank back into the garden, made it into a seat again and sat him down.

"You... you..." he began.

"I know," I said. "I'm foolish."

He shook his head. "You... you... could... have..."

"I could have fired a bigger rock and you would have seen it better," I nodded.

He shook his head. "You... you... could... have... killed me!"

"Sorry, Sir. It was a game I played with my brothers when we were younger. We used to use a small plank to fire balls of cloth in the air and see who could catch them. But I knew it would work for a rock, too."

He glared at me. "Why did you do that?" he demanded.

"Because you told me to get you a rock."
"I did?"
"You did."

"So I did! I was going to show you that it's impossible to throw big rocks at the Roman ships," he said.

"If you say so, Sir," I muttered.

"But if I get a really long plank..."

"As long as a tree," I said.

"As long as a tree... and then I could fire boulders big enough to sink those ships."

I covered my mouth with my hand. "Oh, Sir, that's brilliant! Oh, Sir, I knew you'd invent something to save us! It's true what they say!"

"What *do* they say?"

"That you are the cleverest man in Syracuse!"

Archimedes smiled and nodded. "I am the cleverest man in Greece. In the *world*, in fact!"

CHAPTER 3

You know what happened next, of course. It is written in the history books. Archimedes made his mighty throwing machines – he called them "catapults".

The lord of Syracuse gathered the crowds in the main square. He himself stood at the window of the palace. "The people of Syracuse are blessed by the gods," he cried. "The Romans have their ships and soldiers, but we have Archimedes... the Lion of Syracuse!"

And we all cheered until our throats were sore.

"Roman ships have been sunk," the lord went on (to more cheers), "and the rest have been driven out to sea. All thanks to the great inventor, Archimedes!"

Cheers! More cheers and more.

The next morning, I rose from my straw bed to make my master his breakfast. I found him in the garden, kneeling beside the pond. He was using a toy catapult to fire at toy ships on the pond.

"Would you like breakfast, Sir?" I asked.

He waved me away with a hand. When he was thinking his great thoughts, no one else mattered.

"In the night, the Romans sailed into our harbour under the cloak of darkness," he said quickly.

"So? We can sink them with your great war machines."

He took a pebble and placed it on the toy catapult. "Look... there is a Roman ship in the harbour. I fire a rock."

He fired. The rock landed in the middle of the pond and missed the little ship.

"So? We can move the catapult *back*!" I said.

"I've tried it, simple girl."

He moved the catapult back. He fired again. This time the rock landed on the edge of the pond.

"See?" he groaned. "It landed *on* the harbour. If we get it wrong, we will shatter our own town. The Romans are clever. They know we can't fire at them when they are so close."

I looked at the models and picked up a twig from the garden tree. I took a thread from my tunic and dangled it from the twig. I took a pin and bent it.

"What are you doing, stupid girl?" Archimedes asked.

"When I was a child, I used to fish with my brothers."

I dangled my little rod over the model ship and hooked it into the air. "If the Romans come too close, we could fish them out of the water!" I laughed.

"Idiot child," he snapped. "We cannot build a mighty fishing rod. It's a stupid idea."

"I know, Sir," I sighed.

Archimedes snapped his fingers. "But if we built a tall crane," he murmured, taking the rod from my hand. "We could reach out over the harbour and snatch at the Roman ships. Fix a claw on the end, like a crab's, and snatch them! *Eureka!*"

I covered my mouth with my hand. "Oh, Sir, that's brilliant! Oh, Sir, I knew you'd invent something to save us! It's true what they say!"

"What *do* they say?"

"That you are the cleverest man in Syracuse!"

"We will call it Archimedes' claw!" he nodded.

CHAPTER 4

You will know that Archimedes' claw smashed several Roman ships and drove them back.

Again, the lord of Syracuse gathered the people in the square and told them how great my master was. He paid Archimedes a fortune.

It was strange that his great mind took simple ideas and made them work as weapons of war. Simple games that I used to play as a child. I was too stupid to see how they could help us win the war. But I felt I was sharing in my master's work.

One day, I made a fire using a mirror that bent the sun's rays into a beam of scorching light.

Archimedes watched me and went off muttering.

The next day, my master had built a huge metal mirror that sent a red ray of fire onto the Roman fleet and set their ships alight.

The lord of Syracuse heaped more treasures on my master. I was so proud of him! I suppose, in a way, that is how I killed him. Well, I didn't take his life *myself.* But I was to blame. I was stupid.

You see, the Romans landed in the end. They ran through the town, slaying and avenging.

Finally, they reached our house at the top of the hill. My master was in the garden, planning something new. He was drawing circles in the dust with a stick.

A Roman soldier came up to the gate. "Who lives here?" he asked.

"My master Archimedes, the Lion of Syracuse," I said proudly. And showed him through the garden to where my master was scratching away.

The soldier sighed. "We've heard about him. General Marcellus said he is not to be harmed."

"Ah!" I said. "That's nice. Especially after all he did to you!"

The soldier went stiff. "Did? What do you mean, *did*? He does science and maths and stuff. Harmless, isn't he?"

"Ha! That's good," I laughed. "The great Archimedes invented the catapult that sank your ships."

"My friend died on one of those ships," the soldier growled and pulled his sword free of its sheath.

"Then he invented Archimedes' claw that wrecked more of your ships," I giggled.

"My brother died on one of those ships," the soldier fumed and raised his sword above his head.

"And of course he invented the burning mirror that scorched the rest," I finished.

"I was burned on the arm by that!" the soldier roared. He stepped towards my master. "Archimedes – villain – come with me!"

My master waved him away with a hand. When he was thinking his great thoughts, no one else mattered. Then he said his famous last words: "Don't disturb my circles".

They were his last words because the soldier brought down his sword with the fury of a madman. He spilt my master's mighty brains over those circles in the dust.

ENDINGS

I know. I am stupid.
I should not
have told an
angry soldier
that Archimedes
had invented the
killing machines.
I should have
said, "*I* showed my
master how the
catapult worked. *My*

fishing rod gave him the idea for the
claw. And *my* mirror showed him how to
make a deadly sunbeam."

But the soldier wouldn't believe a stupid

girl could do something like that. Or, here's a chilling thought – maybe he *would* have blamed me. Then he would have killed me!

Maybe being stupid saved my life!

So that is the story of how the Lion of Syracuse died. But what happened to the lion's slave? What happened to me?

You won't be surprised to hear that my master was right – I became a Roman slave. But it's not such a bad life. My new master is kind. In fact, he's far kinder to me than old Archimedes and he *never* calls me stupid!

I only wish my master had shared some of his riches with me before he died. The lord of Syracuse gave him a fortune for his clever machines. I got nothing – although sometimes I think I helped create those inventions.

Still, as Aesop said, "You may share the work of the great, but you will not share the rewards."

And here's another thought: Master Archimedes' reward was a sword in the head. So maybe I can't complain too much.

It was such a pity though. All those fine lion brains that spilled out onto the dusty grass. His circles were disturbed... and the killing spoiled my fine flowers, too.

Such a pity.

EPILOGUE

Aesop's fable

This story draws on 'The Lion's Share'. It tells of a lion, fox, jackal and wolf who, together, kill a stag to eat. They cut it into quarters, but the lion takes every portion – and dares the others to fight him. The fox sees that they may share the work of the great lion, but will not share his rewards.

When someone gets most of something, we still say they get 'the lion's share'.

Aesop

Aesop lived around 2,600 years ago. He left over 600 stories, known as 'fables', which teach lessons.

One book said Aesop was a slave who was freed. Then he carried a message from his king to the people of Delphi. They disliked the message – and threw Aesop off a cliff. As Aesop's fables say, 'it is easier to get into an enemy's troubles than get out again'!

YOU TRY

1. Perfect poetry

The Greeks told many of their greatest stories as poems. The poets would play a musical instrument with strings called a lyre. As they played, they told their tales.

Could you turn 'The Lion's Share' into a poem? It could start:

The fox, the jackal and the wolf
went hunting with the lion.

Together, they could kill a stag
by hardly even tryin'...

You could find some of Aesop's other fables and turn them into poems, too, and then recite them to your friends or family... although you may not be able to play a lyre at the same time.

2. Perfect pictures

Aesop's fables have been told for thousands of years, and are printed in many books. They were written for adults, but are also popular with children. When the tales are printed for young people, they are often illustrated with colourful pictures of the animals. Many have even been made into film and television cartoons.

Can you draw a picture to go with one of Aesop's fables? You could use 'The Lion's Share' or any other one. Underneath your picture, write the lesson learned. For 'The Lion's Share', the lesson is:

'You may share the work of the great, but you will not share the rewards.'